NOT HOME FOR HOLIDAYS

Cyn Bermudez

An imprint of Enslow Publishing

WEST **44** BOOKS™

BROTHERS

TAKEN AWAY   NOT HOME FOR THE HOLIDAYS

THIS PLACE IS NOT MY HOME   JUST MAYBE

Please visit our website, www.west44books.com. For a free color catalog of all our high-quality books, call toll free 1-800-542-2595 or fax 1-877-542-2596.

Cataloging-in-Publication Data

Names: Bermudez, Cyn.
Title: Not home for the holidays / Cyn Bermudez.
Description: New York : West 44, 2020. | Series: Brothers
Identifiers: ISBN 9781538382332 (pbk.) | ISBN 9781538382349 (library bound) | ISBN 9781538383179 (ebook)
Subjects: LCSH: Foster home care--Juvenile fiction. | Electronic mail messages--Juvenile fiction. | Siblings--Juvenile fiction.
Classification: LCC PZ7.B476 No 2019 | DDC [E]--dc23

First Edition

Published in 2020 by
Enslow Publishing LLC
101 West 23rd Street, Suite #240
New York, NY 10011

Copyright © 2020 Enslow Publishing LLC

Editor: Theresa Emminizer
Designer: Sam DeMartin

Photo Credits: cover, title page (gingerbread man) graphicgeoff/Shutterstock.com; front matter (silhouettes) Eladora/Shutterstock.com; p. 31 Maria_Galybina/Shutterstock.com; pp. 47, 68 (trees) strogaya/Shutterstock.com.

Printed in the United States of America

CPSIA compliance information: Batch #CS18W44: For further information contact
Enslow Publishing LLC, New York, New York at 1-800-542-2595.

BROTHERS

PRANKS
FOSTER KEEPERS
PHOTOGRAPHER
VICTOR
YEARBOOK
CAMERA
CASEWORKER
GOBLIN

FOLKLORE

VIOLIN

THANKSGIVING

ISAAC

PHILIPPINES

NEW BABY

CAMOUFLAGE

DUWENDE

COOKING

CHAPTER ONE
The First Signs of Fall

From: isaac-the-great@email.com
To: victory333@email.com
Subject: I'm making stuffing!!!!!

Dad always cooked the turkey. Every Thanksgiving. It was the only thing he knew how to cook. But he was good at it. He made the best turkey. Remember Momma's first time?

It was after Dad died. Our first Thanksgiving without him. Momma had the oven too hot. The turkey was burnt on the outside and raw on the inside. Momma was so sad. She cried a lot. I had never seen Momma cry like that. We ended up eating at Denny's. I was fine with that. You cheered Momma up. You gobbled like a turkey. You made her laugh. I laughed, too. But we also missed Dad so much. Her turkey got better after that. She watched a YouTube video on how to cook turkey.

Now that Momma is in jail, will she get turkey dinner? I hope so. I don't want her to cry.

I wonder how our sisters are doing. Vanessa and Sara cried so much when the cops came. I wish I could email them, too. They're too young for that. I wonder: are their foster keepers like mine or like yours? Don't be mad, but I hope they are more like mine. Like Susan and John. You seem to get bad ones.

I remembered to call Susan and John foster keepers! Just like you said. Not our parents. Just our keepers. Keeping us safe until it's time to go back with Momma. At least I hope.

I can't stop thinking about Susan and John's new baby. The baby will be their first. I don't think she'll want me or Eric when it gets here. They haven't said anything about it. But I'm worried. I can tell Eric is worried, too. He's being extra nice.

Oh, I have something cool to tell you. Stuff you'll like. Last night, Susan told us stories about the little people. Goblins. She called them duwende. That's what they're called where she is from. She grew up in the Philippines. Her mom and dad had a farm in the country. She said little people lived there, too. They stayed mostly invisible. But they like to come out during winter. Sometimes they play pranks, too.

The duwende live out in nature. They live

in trees and burrows. Sometimes, they live under rocks. Or in the small, dark places in a house. In the winter, Susan's parents built the goblins a shelter from the rain. Then the duwende would not play pranks.

John, Eric, and I are going to build a shelter here. For the duwende. John thinks Eric and I should do more together. Help us bond. Since we're both their foster kids. We're making the goblin shelter out of Popsicle sticks. I asked Susan if there are duwende here. She said yes. She said they are everywhere.

I found this site about the duwende: http://www.goblins-around-the-world.com/filipino-duwende-myth.html

Susan told us about her cousins. She said that one time they made a duwende mad. They were playing hide-and-seek. Her youngest cousin forgot to say, "Pardon me." So she got sick. The duwende cursed her cousin. Susan and her other cousins went back and offered fruit. They said, "Please, pardon me." Then she got better. I told Susan the duwende didn't sound nice. She said only if you're not polite. I think I'm polite. I hope.

Thanksgiving is my favorite. Well, Christmas is my favorite. Halloween is my second. Thanksgiving is my third. Momma said, "Stuffing *is* Thanksgiving." Stuffing is the best part. Don't you think? Simple and easy. The turkey depends on it.

I'm making Momma's stuffing for Turkey Day. Susan said I could. Momma taught me last year. First, you cut the bread. Then you toss the bread with a salt mix. Then you dry it. Once the bread is dried, you add broth, butter, and veggies. So far, I've only cut the bread. It's drying right now. You should make it, too. Here's what you need:

- bread
- butter
- broth
- celery

- onions
- salt

I know you don't like to cook. But you should try it. Cooking is super easy. Susan and John are making a turkey. They said it's for me and Eric. Susan usually only makes food from her country: Filipino food. She's making noodles and fish, too. She's also making lots of vegetables. I hope I like it.

I miss Momma. I've been thinking about her a lot. I can't stop wondering what she'll eat for the holiday. Do you think she'll get stuffing? I hope so.

I gotta go now.

TTYS
~Isaac

P.S. We have music classes at my school. It's an elective.

P.P.S. Susan said I can take a music class. But only if I find an instrument for under $100. I'm going to the thrift store. I'm crossing my fingers. Hope I find a violin!

P.P.P.S. I really, really hope I get to take a music class!

P.P.P.P.S. Love you, bro!

3 Attachments:

Popsicle-sticks.jpg

I-drew-a-duwende.jpg

Bread-drying-for-stuffing.jpg

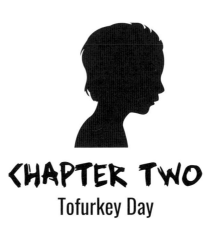

CHAPTER TWO
Tofurkey Day

From: victory333@email.com
To: isaac-the-great@email.com
Subject: Happy Thanksgiving!

Ha ha! I remember that Thanksgiving. The turkey was so burnt. The hardest part was Dad being gone. Now they are both gone. Not in the same way. But it's like you said. We're all separated. And I hope Momma has turkey and stuffing, too.

I got a letter from Momma. I'm writing her a letter back. You should, too. I miss her. A lot.

Thanksgiving and Christmas won't be the same. It was hard when it was just Dad gone. Now…

I hope we get to see Momma at Christmastime. I actually said a prayer. But I'm not betting on it. Just like I don't believe the caseworker. Or my new foster keeper, Rachel. Or my other foster keeper, Lin. Though they are better than my last keepers. And the boys' home, too.

I'm not mad. I hope Vanessa and Sara's foster keepers are good, too. I hope this foster home sticks until Momma gets out. There are rules here, too. They're kinda strict. Lights out is at ten. But they have a computer. I'm not limited with my time anymore. That's nice. I'm at the same school with my best friend Lucky. So I can't complain.

But like I said. I'm not getting my hopes up. Momma took so long to write us. And things just don't work like that. Not for us. Seems that way. I'm just happy she wrote us. I miss her so much. Sometimes I'm afraid Vanessa and Sara will forget her. They're only five and six. That's younger than we were when Dad died. I try to remember Dad's face without looking at a picture. The image in my head has faded. More as time passes. I look at a picture, and it's like a dream. The memory of him is hazy and faded.

Anyway. I don't want to be a bummer.

There are two other kids here. Both of them are older than me. They don't really talk to me much. Rachel and Lin have a big house. There's a yard. I even have my own room. It's okay, I guess. Like I said, there is a computer we can all use. We just have to sign up to use it. But we can use it up to two hours. Rachel and Lin have a lot of pictures. The pictures are all over the walls. A lot of kids. Probably the foster kids that used to live here. Rachel also volunteers at the boys' home.

We eat a lot of organic foods. Tofu and lentils. Rachel and Lin don't eat meat. We're not eating traditional Thanksgiving dinner. We're having tofurkey. It's a fake turkey made of tofu!

Weird, huh? More than that. They don't eat anything that comes from an animal. So no milk or cheese. The food isn't that bad though. Some of it tastes pretty good. Lin is a good cook. She makes good soup. Rachel bakes good cookies. Not as good as Momma's. Or yours!

Oh, you know what you should make—Momma's Christmas cookies! Maybe we can bring some to Momma. If we get to see her. Decorate the cookies, too. The way you and Momma do every Christmas. Like little gingerbread men.

I almost forgot! I have good news, too. Two things, actually. I'm the new photographer for the school newspaper. *And* the yearbook. Lucky showed our English teacher some of my pictures. The ones I take for fun. I take photos of everyone. Especially at school. She liked my photos! She said I have a "good eye." That I have talent. So this will be a lot of fun. Cool, huh? I'm excited. I'm…happy. As happy as I can be…

Is it wrong to feel this way?

Anyway, Lucky writes articles for the school paper. I told him about your goblin problem—the duwende. He's going to do a piece on goblin folklore. He said many countries have goblin-like creatures. He said Mexico does, too. He said they are either good or bad. Helpers or tricksters. What kind live there with you and your foster keepers? I hope they are helpers.

Hey, I have a plan. We should try and capture one. Or at least take pictures of them! The Polaroid John gave you would work fine. Then we can sell them to make money or get famous. Then maybe we could get Momma out of jail. Or at least buy her a really good Christmas gift.

Lucky and I are game for the capture! How about Saturday? The duwende are everywhere. They will be here, too. Right? I'll have Dad's old camera. I'll take pictures, too. I read the web page at the link you sent. The website said goblins like raspberry-lemon macarons. I'm not sure if that's right information. But I think we can start with that. To lure them in. I will research different types of traps. I'm thinking something like a rabbit trap.

Anyway. I have to get going. I have to help set the table. I'm on silverware duty.

Happy Thanksgiving, lil bro.
Victor

P.S. I didn't make stuffing. I can't cook! Hahahaha

1 Attachment:
Raspberry-Lemon-Macarons.jpg

CHAPTER THREE
Autumn Plans

From: isaac-the-great@email.com
To: victory333@email.com
Subject: Let's do it!

What are you writing in your letter? I'm going to write one, too. This is my first time writing a letter by hand. John said it was a good thing. He said most people don't write by hand these days. He said handwritten letters are more meaningful.

John and Susan used to write letters to each other. When they were younger. He showed them to me. They both kept their letters. They were so old. The paper was worn and falling apart. I thought they were neat to look at. John said I should handwrite letters more often. He said it would be a good outlet.

I'm writing one for the caseworker. John agreed that it was a good idea. I just want to tell her one thing. About how much we want to see Momma for Christmas. John said he will mail it today. As soon as I finish it.

I know you don't want to hope. But I do. I hope. I'm hopeful we will see Momma.

I didn't say anything to John or Susan. I want to write them a letter, too. I'm hopeful about Momma. But I'm stressing about the new baby. I know they won't wanna keep foster kids around. And I don't blame them. It makes sense. They'll have their own kid to take care of. I've been having trouble sleeping. I can't stop thinking about it!

That's why I kind of like your duwende

plan. I know we were wrong about the werewolf and ghost before. And maybe our imaginations are crazy. But really, I just need a distraction. So I don't have to think about the new baby. Or how I might have to move.

Just remember, Susan said the duwende like politeness. Trying to take pictures doesn't seem polite. Trying to capture one definitely doesn't seem polite. If you're not polite, the duwende will curse you. I don't want to be cursed. I don't want you to be cursed, either. What if you make them mad? Just be careful. Maybe it's a bad idea? But I mean, it would be kinda cool…

My friend Stephanie thinks we should. She just wants proof. She said she has to see one with her own eyes. Otherwise, it's not real. I said, you can't see electricity. And that's real. She said that was different.

"How?" I asked.

I said, you believe in God. You can't see him.

She said that was different, too. But she wouldn't tell me how! Still, we talked about your plan. Let's do it! But we're supposed to say "pardon me" when they are near. So remember to say that. Tell Lucky, too.

Okay. Tell me what the next steps are. Stephanie liked your rabbit trap idea. She said it would be easy to make. I already got a box. It's cardboard. I painted it forest green. For camouflage. That way the box blends in with the grass. Next, I need to make some kind of trench. Or place I can hide with my Polaroid.

So cool about the photography thing! Your pictures *are* good. I've told you that before. I'm glad things are better for you. So…it sounds like your new foster keepers are better than your last ones. Every place has rules. Momma had rules, too.

I hope Momma had a good Thanksgiving dinner.

That reminds me. Tofurkey? That sounds

super weird. Aren't you starving? My stuffing was delicious! We had pancit (Filipino noodles), lumpia (Filipino eggrolls), turkey, ham, and my stuffing. It was really good. And there were so many pies. Pumpkin and apple and rhubarb. Susan made this Filipino drink called halo-halo. It's made with coconut and jackfruit.

It's time for dinner. I gotta go wash up. We're having leftovers. Lots of leftovers. I wish I could give you some.

TTYS

~Isaac

P.S. Yes! I'll make Christmas cookies. Enough for you, Momma, and our sisters!

2 Attachments:

Green-Camouflage-Box.jpg

John's-stack-of-handwritten-letters.jpg

CHAPTER FOUR
Fog Delays

From: victory333@email.com
To: isaac-the-great@email.com
Subject: School started late today!

This fog is crazy! School started at ten today. I wish we always started at ten. I like sleeping in.

Hey, I'm glad you're writing Momma, too. I'm just writing about how we might see her. Also about how I'm doing. None of the bad stuff. Like getting in trouble. Or moving around to different foster homes. I don't want to worry her. Only the good stuff. Like meeting Lucky. And being the photographer for the school newspaper. Eating tofurkey. That last one isn't good stuff. It isn't bad stuff, either.

The tofurkey tasted okay. I ate pie, too. The food was good. Not as good as Momma's. Rachel's parents came.

I have a Christmas list, too. Rachel and Lin asked all the kids to make one. They said to list three things we really want. I don't want anything like action figures or games. But since I had to, here is my list:

1. See Momma.

2. See Isaac, Vanessa, and Sara.

3. Pizza

Anyway. Here is the plan. We're going to make raspberry-lemon macarons. Good start on the rabbit trap. Lucky and I thought that was a good idea. We are doing the same. We are going to paint our box green, too. We'll prop the box up with a stick. Tie a string around the stick. We'll place the macarons on a plate. The plate goes under the box. Then we'll hide in the bushes and wait.

When a duwende comes by, he will want to eat the macarons. When he does, we'll pull the string. Fast!

When you do it, Stephanie should be in charge of the string. You hide with your Polaroid. Snap a picture when Stephanie pulls the string. Lucky and I will do the same on our field trip. The forest should have a lot of duwende. Especially if they like nature.

Here is what you need for the macarons:
- powdered sugar
- almond flour
- egg whites
- pinch of salt
- sugar
- red food coloring

Here is what you need for the raspberry-lemon curd:

- raspberries
- egg yolks
- powdered sugar
- lemon juice
- lemon zest
- butter

Here is the link for the instructions: http://www.macaron-mania.com/raspberry-lemon-macaron.html

Can you imagine if we caught one? Or even just take a picture? We will be famous. Maybe even rich. We can buy Momma a house. We'll definitely be on TV.

Now you just have to pick a day. I think we should try on Saturday. Lucky is sleeping over. We'll get up at six in the morning. I'll be ready. I'll take a lot of pictures.

Anyway. I'm going to go to the store and get the rest of the supplies.

TTYS

Victor

P.S. Writing a letter to your keepers is a good idea. They should tell you what's up. So you don't worry. Anyway, keep me posted.

1 Attachment

Tofurkey.jpg

CHAPTER FIVE
Faded Memories

From: isaac-the-great@email.com
To: victory333@email.com
Subject: Yay macarons!

You are going to bake?! No way! I wish I could be there to see it. I hope you like baking. Then we can cook and bake together for Momma. When we all go home. Maybe?

Susan heard back from the caseworker. We are going to see Momma on Christmas Eve! I'm so excited. I have a lot of Christmas cookies to make.

I made the first batch of macarons. Stephanie and I taste-tested them. They are yummy! Stephanie and I will make more Friday night. She's coming over to hang out. So it will be a perfect time.

Hey…I wanted to remind you. Please be careful. I don't want you to get in trouble again. Not just with the duwende. But with your foster keepers, too.

Stephanie said I should tell Susan our plans. She said Susan should know. But what if she doesn't want us to capture a duwende? Susan told me about her cousin. She got REALLY sick. John told me more stories from his town. He grew up in the Philippines, too. He said the duwende like to play pranks. He said they like to take things. Sometimes even kids!

At school, I told my teacher about them. My teacher's name is Mr. Gomez. He said it was interesting. He said I should write about them, too. For our social studies report. Goblin folklore around the world. Or folklore of the Philippines.

I told Mr. Gomez about Lucky. That Lucky is writing an article for the school paper. He said I could cite Lucky. That means give credit for something someone else wrote.

Susan's belly is getting bigger. Susan and John are starting to prepare. They are getting everything ready for the baby. They are having a girl. John painted the nursery green and pink. There's already a crib in there. A rocking chair and a dresser, too.

I wrote the letter, but I hid it. I don't know if I should say anything. I don't want to upset Susan. She's been crying. Something sad happened. Susan's mother died. I feel sad for her. I think decorating for the baby helped Susan feel a little better.

Susan's mother dying made me think about Dad. I think a lot at night. In the dark, when everyone is asleep. You wrote that you don't remember Dad's face much anymore. It's the same for me. But even worse because I was younger. I have lots of memories of him. Like the way he cooked turkey. But I can't remember his eyes. I can't remember his nose. Or his mouth. When we were at home, I'd look at his pictures. I needed them to fill in his face. But now there are no pictures. They're all in storage.

What if our sisters forget Momma? What if Vanessa and Sara forget us, too?! I hope they don't. I asked Susan if they will be there. When we go visit Momma in jail. She said she thinks so.

Do you ever dream about Momma? I do. Susan said it's because I miss her.

It's late. I have to go to bed now.

TTYS

~Isaac

P.S. I only wrote Momma good stuff, too.

P.P.S. Susan said I could bake Christmas cookies.

1 Attachment:

My-Macarons.jpg

CHAPTER SIX
Falling Leaves

From: victory333@email.com
To: isaac-the-great@email.com
Subject: Let's catch a goblin!

I'm not baking! Lucky is making the macarons. Actually, I think his mom is. I already told my foster keeper my plan.

I said, "Lucky and I are going to catch a goblin."

She asked me where. I said in the backyard. She said, "Don't dig holes in the backyard. Or disturb my garden."

I said I wouldn't. She looked at me sort of funny. She said, "You know, goblins are not a protected species." Then she smiled and said, "Just don't do anything illegal."

Lucky's mom said there was no such thing as goblins. I asked Lucky what he thought. He said, "We hunted a werewolf. Sort of. And a ghost. A goblin is just as real."

I guess he's kind of right. But the werewolf wasn't a werewolf. Just an old man. And the ghost…I think we can debate that one.

I asked the other two foster kids. Jody, the oldest, laughed. She said I was crazy. Jody is tall and dark-skinned. She's really skinny. She's going to be 18 in January. Then she is out of foster care and on her own. She is a senior this year. I asked her what she'll do. Jody said she's not sure. I wonder what happened with her parents. I didn't ask that. I don't like it when people ask about

Momma. So I don't ask, either.

The other foster kid, Raymond, said maybe. He said anything is possible. He said that sometimes made-up things end up being real. Raymond is not too tall but not short, either. He is chubby. His cheeks shake when he laughs. He is always laughing. He will be 18 next year.

I like the other foster kids. They don't bother me much. They don't ask me questions. Or tease me. Okay, Jody called me crazy. But just once.

It's really quiet here. Except for the music. But the music usually is not loud. It's weird music. Only instruments. Are you playing an instrument? Did you find a violin?

Anyway. There are a lot of crystals in this house, too.

I'm so glad we're going to see Momma. Thanksgiving wasn't the same. Christmas without her would really stink! But now we can at least see her.

Momma loves Christmas cookies. I'm glad you're making them. I need to do something special, too. No, I'm not baking. I think I'll make her something. Or maybe buy her something. I started saving soda cans. And plastic bottles. There is a recycle station nearby. Rachel drives me there. I've made ten bucks so far! A neighbor said I could help with his lawn. He said he'd give me five dollars an hour. Can Momma have gifts in jail? I'll ask.

Yes, I dream of Momma. I think about her, too. I hope she's okay. I hope she has food. I hope no one is mean to her. I think about her face, her eyes. I don't want to forget. So I think about her all the time. I hate that we're separated. I hate it. As nice as Rachel and Lin are, they are not my family.

Christmas is a couple of weeks away. We have a lot to do. Not just for visiting Momma. But for our goblin plan. Saturday is the day!

I have to go now. Talk to you soon.

Victor

P.S. I hope you found a violin. Momma would love you playing an instrument.

P.P.S. Give John the letter. Let him read it first.

1 Attachment:

Crystals.jpg

CHAPTER SEVEN
The Goblin Cat

From: isaac-the-great@email.com
To: victory333@email.com
Subject: You won't believe what happened!

Stephanie came over around dinnertime. Around 7:00. We ate. We waited for it to get dark. Then Susan and John started to watch TV. Right on cue. We had an hour before John would take Stephanie home.

I had decided not to say anything to Susan and John. John wanted to make the duwende shelter. So I didn't think they would want us to capture one. We snuck out fast.

We set up the box outside. Just like we said. Stephanie held the string. We hid on the side of the house. We wore all black. Stephanie brought brown and green makeup. I said no way. She said it was camouflage. We put brown and green makeup on our faces. Like soldiers in the movies. I had my camera ready. She had the string in her hands.

There was a dog howling. It sounded far away. The neighbor's cat started to cry. The cat sounded like a baby! Then the dog howled more! Then another dog started barking. Stephanie signaled for me to stay quiet. It was scary.

That's when I saw it.

Okay, I'm not sure what I saw. The wind started to blow harder. Leaves flew in the air. A lot of them. They swirled around. A few even whipped me in the cheek. Then Stephanie screamed! I started yelling. Something ran past us. It was blurry. And fast. It could have been the neighbor's cat.

"Pardon me. Pardon me!"

I said it over and over. Somehow, I snapped a picture. A bright flash blinded me. Stephanie tried to run. She slipped in the mud. She accidentally pushed me over. Then I fell to the ground. It all happened so fast.

Well, we alerted Susan and John. All the lights in the house came on. Everybody came downstairs and then outside. Susan looked worried at first. She asked if Stephanie and I were okay. I said yes. We all went back into the house.

Inside the house, Stephanie and I sat on the sofa. Susan looked upset. John had a smile on his face. Susan asked me what were doing. I told her we were trying to capture the duwende. She asked me why. I said because we could be rich. Then John started laughing. Susan gave John a mad look. He stopped laughing.

"I said 'pardon me,'" I said to Susan.

"Did you catch it?" John asked.

I shook my head no. I felt so bad. They didn't yell at us, though. Susan said not to do that again. She got mad at John for laughing. She said the duwende are not superstition. Not to her family. John apologized. John told me no more goblin hunting. They sent me to my room. John brought Stephanie home.

That night, I waited for everyone to fall asleep. I tiptoed downstairs. I picked up the Polaroid picture. I had left it on the coffee table. I took the picture upstairs to my room. I didn't turn on the light. Because that would wake Susan. I took out a flashlight instead. I got under the covers and shined the light on the picture.

You know what I saw?! The neighbor's darn cat. I got an up-close shot of her face. An orange cat with bright green eyes! Can you believe it?! All that work for nothing!

Maybe you and Lucky will have better luck. Maybe there are no duwende.

I better go. I'm not in trouble. But Susan isn't happy about what I did.

~Isaac

P.S. I think you're right. John should read the letter first. If I decide to give it to them. Right now, I don't think it's a good idea.

1 Attachment:
Goblin-Cat.jpg

CHAPTER EIGHT
The Goblin Night

From: victory333@email.com
To: isaac-the-great@email.com
Subject: Don't be mad, I forgot!

Rachel and Lin have a big backyard. But Lucky and I thought we should try a different place. We walked down to the park. It's a big park, lots of trees. And there is a creek, too. We walked about a mile away. We went in the middle of the night. Like 3:00. I'm not sure.

The air was cold and misty. I felt damp air

on my legs and arms. Even through my pants and sweater. I had a thick jacket on, too. I could see my breath. My cheeks stung. My ears were red. And my lips were dry.

Lucky and I found a spot. There was a huge tree.

We spotted a large hole in the trunk of the tree. I thought a goblin must be in there. Lucky agreed. We set up the camera. We hid it behind a boulder by the river. It was the perfect spot. There were a lot of bushes in front of the boulder. We were well hidden. But we could also see the tree.

We waited and waited. Seemed like forever. At the park, the sky was extra dark. Only one park light was on. I thought that was good. That maybe the duwende would come out for sure. I think Lucky was scared. He paced back and forth. He kept looking at his phone. And he kept looking at the park light.

He pointed at the light and said, "Maybe we

should go over there where it's not so dark."

But dark is the whole point! We kept hearing things. Crickets chirping. Dogs barking. Birds singing. I didn't know birds sang at night! The leaves rustled. It sounded like footsteps on the grass. Soon we heard cars, too. Starting. Or their alarms. We whipped our heads in the direction of the different sounds. I took pictures even though I couldn't see anything. Sometimes, it felt like something moved past me. I'd feel the wind shift. But in the end, we caught nothing. We saw nothing.

The sun came up. Lucky and I were tired. We'd been up most of the night. We decided to call it quits. People started walking their dogs in the park. We packed up and walked back to my foster home. Lin was awake. Rachel was still asleep. I was worried at first. I had told Rachel we were going goblin hunting. But I said we were going to be in the backyard. I hadn't decided differently at that time.

But when I walked in, Lin only said, "How'd it go?"

I asked, "What?"

She said, "Did you catch a goblin?" She took a sip of her coffee.

"No," I said.

I was disappointed. I think she knew.

There were cookies on the counter. Lucky and I sat at the kitchen table. We ate some cookies. Soon, everyone else woke up. Rachel asked about the duwende. She asked if I remembered to say, "Pardon me."

"How did you know I was supposed to say that?" I asked.

"Everyone knows," she said and smiled.

Well, I didn't know. I mean, you told me, but I didn't before that. Anyway. I forgot!!!! I didn't say "pardon me." Is something going to happen to me? Or to Lucky?

I looked at the pictures I took. There was nothing there. Except for one. It's blurry. You can't really see anything. But there's a shape. It's not a cat. Or a dog. Or a bird. What do you think it is?!

Anyway, I have homework to do.

TTYS

Victor

P.S. Just do it!! Give John the letter!

1 Attachment:

What-is-this-?.jpg

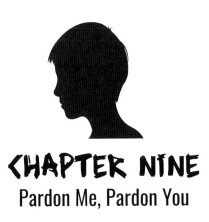

CHAPTER NINE
Pardon Me, Pardon You

From: isaac-the-great@email.com
To: victory333@email.com
Subject: Oh no!

Our visit to Momma might be canceled. She got sick. Do you think it's because of the duwende? I do. You forgot to say "pardon me." But *you* were supposed to get sick. Or Lucky. Or both of you. Not Momma. What are we going to do? We have to see her.

The duwende cursed us. I just know it. First,

Momma got sick. Then I lost the letter to John and Susan.

Then John found it! I forgot it in my coat pocket. He was getting my clothes ready for the laundry. He hasn't said anything to me. About the letter. Neither has Susan. And she can see how stressed out I am! She just thinks it's because of Momma. But I know they have my letter.

Susan said not to worry about Momma. She feels sad for me. I mean, she's extra sad because her mom died. Susan's mom's name was Juliana. We went to her funeral yesterday. There were a lot of people there. And photos of Susan with her mom. They were taken when Susan was a kid. There were white roses, too.

It reminded me of Dad's funeral. Kind of like not real. Like a dream. But I also felt weird being there. Like I didn't belong there. Like it should have been private. For only Susan and John. Then when we got home, the caseworker called.

She told Susan we might not see Momma. Because Momma had gotten sick. Susan cried! She said it was important that we see her.

I try not to think about it. All the sadness. I've been working on my report. And praying, too. John said to stay positive. He said to have faith. Christmas will be here soon. I'm going to get everything I need for the Christmas cookies. Just in case.

You should see the Christmas tree here. Susan and John bought a big one. All the different ornaments are pretty. I like the colored lights, too. There is a huge angel on top. I like it. But also, I can't be completely happy. It feels like a kind of home. But it's not home. And if I enjoy myself, does that mean I'm betraying Momma?

Remember that one Christmas when Momma bought a huge tree? She wanted to cheer us up after Dad died. We always got a short, fat one before. Momma loved garlands. Red, green, and gold. The tree looked like it wore a fuzzy sweater. And the lights…Momma got the wrong ones. The big ones that go outside. We teased her about it. But we still put them on the tree.

Momma was so happy she got a big tree. But then we couldn't get new ornaments. There wasn't enough money.

I miss Momma and you and our sisters. I miss everything. I miss the house. The way the house smelled at Christmas. It smelled like pine. There is a pine smell here, too. But it's not the same. Nothing is the same without Momma.

Do you think that's why Momma stole that money? So she could get us big Christmas trees all the time? I wish she would have asked us first. I would rather have the short, fat trees. I'd rather have Momma. I don't care about having a Christmas tree.

Truthfully, it doesn't feel like Christmas without Momma. Or without you and Vanessa and Sara.

How is Christmas over there? Did your foster keepers buy a Christmas tree?

I'll make a lot of cookies. Enough for everyone. Just in case. I'll even make extra for good luck! You can bring some to Lucky. I have to leave now. I'm going to the store to pick up the ingredients:

- butter
- sugar
- eggs
- vanilla
- flour
- baking soda
- salt

Talk to you soon, bro.

~ Isaac

P.S. Send pictures of your tree!

P.P.S. Do you feel cursed?

1 Attachment

Look-at-this-huge-christmas-tree.jpg

CHAPTER TEN
Not Home For Christmas

From: victory333@email.com
To: isaac-the-great@email.com
Subject: I need fruit!

Sorry I'm just getting back to you. I've been sick. So is Lucky. I've been barfing for the past couple of days. Lin said I caught the flu. That I must have caught it that night. The night of our plan. She said that's why Lucky is sick, too. So great! I didn't catch a duwende. But I caught a flu!

I told Lucky about what you said. How the

duwende probably cursed us. Maybe that's why I'm sick. Lucky said the flu was going around. So we're probably not sick because of the goblins. I said we should bring the goblins fruit anyway. What kind of fruit do I bring? The website you sent said "oranges, apples, and more." What exactly is "more"? Like, any fruit? Like, can I bring a tomato? Tomatoes are fruit.

That's a pretty Christmas tree. I love it. Rachel and Lin don't celebrate Christmas. They celebrate Winter Solstice. But they have a Christmas tree, too. Except their tree is a living tree. They don't buy one that is chopped down. The tree is in a pot. After Christmas, they will plant the tree. Cool, huh? It's small. It's a baby tree. But I like the idea. Giving the tree life is good.

Still, it's not *our* tradition. And it's not

Christmas without our old traditions. We can't enjoy ourselves too much. Or we'll forget what we had.

I miss our short, fat Christmas trees, too. Momma always made Mexican chocolate milk. The smell of cinnamon mixed with the smell of pine. You know what else I miss? Tamales.

I used to hate having to wrap tamales. Momma always asked me to help. Because I'm the oldest. Now, I would love to sit at the table making tamales. Because I'd be next to Momma. I'd rather have all those days back. I don't care about the money either. I don't know why Momma did what she did. I wish she hadn't. She should have talked to us first.

Rachel talked to me about choice at dinner. It was the other day. I don't remember how the topic came up. She said every choice we make has an effect.

Like what Momma did. She made a choice.

She did something bad. It's not just her who's paying for it. All of us are. Me, you, and our sisters. So we should think about our choices. And how they could affect others. Not just ourselves. That way we can make good choices.

Rachel said the caseworker called. She said there is a chance we might be able to visit Momma! She is being treated. She is getting better. We will find out tomorrow. *crossing fingers*

Maybe it'll be a Christmas miracle? I got Momma a gift. It's from all of us. It's a picture of me, you, Vanessa, and Sara. I had one in my camera. I bought a nice, pretty frame. That way Momma will have us with her.

I can't wait to eat the cookies!

Anyway. I'm super tired! My body hurts. Especially my throat.

Hey, seriously. Let me know about the fruit. I don't know if my keepers will let me go back to the park. At least not while I'm sick. I said, "What's the point then?" After will be too late. If there is an after. The point of the fruit is to give it before.

Okay. I gotta get some sleep.

TTYS

Love you too, lil bro.

Victor

P.S. I'll try to keep hoping. That I'll get better. That Momma will get better. That we'll get to see her. And we'll be a family again for Christmas.

1 Attachment:

Yule-tree.jpg

CHAPTER ELEVEN
Goblin Fruit

From: isaac-the-great@email.com
To: victory333@email.com
Subject: Yay—we're going to see Momma!

We get to see Momma. I can't wait! And we get to see each other. I made a ton of cookies. They are gingerbread men. I tried to make them smile really big. Susan said it was thoughtful. She said it was funny, too. Funny in a good way.

Oh, before I forget. Everything we bring has to be approved. I already talked to the caseworker.

She said it's okay to bring the cookies. But you can't bring the frame. Did she tell you yet? Maybe make a paper frame. Can I have a copy of the picture, too?

I hope you're feeling better. I don't know what fruit to give angry duwende. I asked Susan. She said jackfruit. It's really spiky. Or maybe coconut. I don't think that's helpful. I don't know where you could buy those. I said, "Pardon me." In a prayer. For you and Lucky and Momma. That way, the duwende in the house would hear me. Maybe it worked? Momma did get better.

I said a prayer for everyone. Even Susan and John. I don't want Susan to be sad anymore. She cries for her mom. I cry for Momma, too. But at night. Alone in my bed. Where no one can see or hear me. Sometimes, I want to tell Susan things will get better. She told me that, too. When I first came here.

Also, her belly is getting bigger and bigger. I asked her how big it will get. She giggled and said, "As big as a football field."

I asked, "Seriously?" I really wanted to know. But she didn't answer me. Momma got big when she was pregnant with Sara. But not *that* big.

Winter is here. Outside, the air looks white. Remember when we went on that family trip to Yosemite? We went on Christmas vacation. It was very cold. There was snow. A lot of snow.

That's why Dad took us there. He and Momma wanted us to see the snow. Momma loved the snow. Remember how we made snow angels? We'd lie down in the snow. Then we'd flap our hands and legs.

Oh, and the snowman!!! We built a snowman. Dad had the "Frosty the Snowman" song on. The song blared from the car radio. We used raisins for the eyes and mouth. A carrot for the nose. I would love to see those pictures. They're in storage, though.

Then when we left, it started to snow. There was a lot of snowfall. We couldn't see anything. Driving home was scary. We couldn't see past the hood of the car. Dad drove like three miles per hour. Momma kept reminding Dad about the cliff. Dad said to stop side-seat driving. But we made it home okay. Obviously. But once we got out of the snow, we hugged. Everyone hugged so tight. Momma said we were never going back there. Well, not during the cold season.

I think I'm too excited to sleep. But I need to try. My stuff is packed. I'm ready for the drive. I'm going to bed now.

See you soon!!!

Love you, bro.

~ Isaac

P.S. Don't forget your camera. I will bring mine, too. That way we can take a lot of pictures.

P.P.S. We should bring something for Vanessa and Sara. Besides the cookies!

P.P.P.S. Maybe the same picture for everyone?

P.P.P.P.S. I finally found a violin! Just in time. I am going to take music lessons! Can you believe it?

P.P.P.P.P.S. I think the curse is broken!

3 Attachments:

Jack-fruit-looks-alien.jpg

I-drew-a-snow-man.jpg

Big-box-of-cookies.jpg

CHAPTER TWELVE
A Christmas Visit

From: victory333@email.com
To: isaac-the-great@email.com
Subject: Merry Christmas!

Momma looked different. Right? Smaller than usual. Skinny. Her uniform looked loose. Her face looked sunken. Dark circles under her eyes. Maybe it was the visitor's area. The lights in there were too white. Made everything look stale. Colorless. Still, Momma was too thin. I hope she is eating.

One time, I had gotten sick. Like really sick. I don't know if you remember. Dad was still alive. But he wasn't home. He was working late. I was in bed. My head was hurting. My chest was hurting. I could hardly breathe. I had a fever, too. I kept tossing and turning. I couldn't sleep. All of a sudden, it got hard to breathe. I went to Momma. She was still up. She was in the kitchen. She was sitting at the kitchen table. I think she was paying bills. She had her checkbook opened. She saw me. Her face went pale. She grabbed me quickly. She held me over the sink. She stuck her finger in my throat. I threw up all over! But after that I could breathe again. She always knew what to do. I wish I knew what to do. How I can help her. But I don't.

I miss Momma's hugs. I didn't want to let go of her the other day. I just wanted to hug her tight. She still smells the same. Like strawberries and soap. It seemed to take forever to see her. But then the time went by fast.

My favorite part of the whole visit was Momma's singing. She always sang us that song. When we were little. When it was time to sleep. She held all of us this time! Well, I stood with her arm around me. Do you know the lyrics in English?

Something like, "Sleep my baby. Sleep my love." It sounds better in Spanish.

Mom touched your face. You have bags under your eyes from not sleeping. That's why she asked, "Everything okay?" I wanted to ask her the same thing.

Did you hear Sara? She whispered, "When you coming home?"

My chest felt heavy when she said it. Vanessa nudged Sara with her elbow.

Vanessa said, "Don't ask things like that."

Momma said it was okay. That's when she said, "Always tell me your thoughts. Always tell me your feelings. I love you no matter what."

I asked, "You'll love us even if we're not sad all the time while you're gone?"

She said, "No matter what. I want you to be happy." That made me feel better. Like I can relax. I looked at you and I think you felt the same.

You've grown! So have Vanessa and Sara. You look taller. I bet you'd pass me on The Wall at home. The wall where we mark our height. You're as tall as me! Almost. I bet The Wall isn't there anymore. Painted over. Probably painted white. I don't know. I wonder what happened to our apartment. Like I wonder who lives there. Do they have kids? I think about it a lot.

Sometimes, I try to wish really hard. Like maybe things will go back. I want to be normal again. A normal family. Doing normal things.

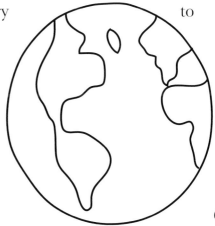

Rachel said we cannot go back. Only forward. I don't like the sound of that. We don't know where forward is.

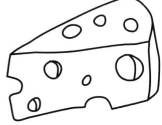

But it made me think. So I tried to enjoy myself on Christmas Day. I took pictures of everything new.

Rachel and Lin got us gifts. I got a globe. It's cool. About the size of a basketball. I'm taking my time. I'm going through each country. I want to know each place. At least two facts.

Did you know the kids in France eat cheese for lunch? Every day! Or the kids in Japan make and serve their own school lunch? And I thought Pizza Friday was cool. One day, I'll tell Momma all the things I've learned. And she'll be proud.

I gotta go now. I'm super tired. And I'm stuffed. All we had were vegetable dishes for Christmas. They were actually kind of good. Especially the sweets. The pie was PURPLE.

Oh, I'm feeling a lot better. So I guess no goblins. Right?

I love you, lil bro.
TTYS
Victor

P.S. You found a violin! That's cool. If I could play an instrument, I'd play the piano. Or guitar. I want to hear you play. Record yourself on the computer.

3 Attachments
Globe.jpg
Christmas-Vegetable-Dinner.jpg
Purple-Yam-Pie.jpg

CHAPTER THIRTEEN
A Winter Wish

From: isaac-the-great@email.com
To: victory333@email.com
Subject: Re: Merry Christmas!

Seeing Momma was the best Christmas present ever. And you and our sisters. I didn't want the visit to end.

When you took Sara to the bathroom, Momma hugged Vanessa and me tight.

Momma said, "Come here, my babies."

Vanessa started crying. Then I started

crying. Then Momma started crying. Momma kept saying, "I'm so sorry."

I said, "Momma, it's okay. We love you, too. No matter what."

She hugged us tighter and said "No more tears" in Spanish.

Momma did look skinny. I hope she's okay, too. You're right. Momma always knew what to do. Before jail.

Susan said not to worry. Because worrying doesn't change anything. Worrying just makes you sick. And sad. So why waste time like that? I think good thoughts. John said that's how to be hopeful. Think positive. I want you to stay hopeful, too. John said memories are positive.

I asked, "Even the sad ones?"

He said yes. He said our memories shape us. I'm not sure what that means. I think it means who we are. How we think. What we love. What we hate. John said Momma is always with us. She's with us because of our memories. We can move forward, because we'll always have our memories.

Anyway…Christmas!

I can't believe you ate purple yam pie!!! I've never seen pie that purple before. I don't how all vegetables can be good. Maybe you're just used to it. We had a huge Christmas dinner. It was a Christmas party at the community center. It wasn't like any Christmas we ever had. But it wasn't bad, either.

There were a lot of people at the party. There was a roasted pig! The pig had an apple in its mouth. It looked scary. Susan said to try it. She said tasting the pork was the only way to know. She said I might like it. I did! The pork tasted good. My favorite part of dinner was the sweet rice.

We opened gifts too. I got a sweater. It's green and red.

And has a Christmas tree on it. I said I liked it.
But…well, I don't want to wear it. I will, though.
Susan made it. I'd feel bad if I didn't.

Oh, and Susan and John spoke to me about
my letter. Finally.

Susan and John said they are not sending
me and Eric away. Susan said
not to worry about that. She
promised. Even with the
baby. She'll still take care
of me. That makes me feel
hopeful.

Well, I'm off
to practice the violin.
Stephanie said my playing
sounded bad. Like a crying cat.

I said, "Hey, I'm new to this."

She just laughed at me. I recorded my
playing. Like you asked. So I'm warning you. My
violin playing may hurt your ears.

Love you too, bro.

~Isaac

P.S. I like your globe!

P.P.S. No more goblin adventures. No more duwende. I know there aren't any. But just in case.

P.P.P.S. Stay hopeful! We will be normal again. Next Christmas.

P.P.P.P.S. What is normal? John said there was no such thing. I just want to be us again. That's my Christmas wish.

3 Attachments

My-Violin.jpg

Christmas-Sweater.jpg

Roasted-Pig.jpg

Want to Keep Reading?

Turn the page for a sneak peek at
the next book in the series.

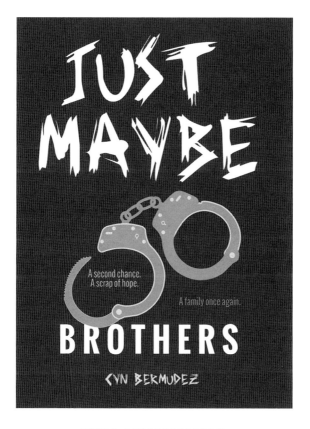

ISBN: 9781538382356

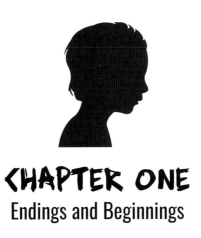

CHAPTER ONE
Endings and Beginnings

From: victory333@email.com
To: isaac-the-great@email.com
Subject: New Foster Keepers

Sunsets remind me of Momma. It was her favorite time of day. She loved the colors. The way the colors hugged the horizon. The way orange covered the sky. Like spilled paint across a light-blue canvas.

Momma once said, "Sunsets are like God's reset button. No matter your mistakes. The sun sets, and tomorrow you start new. Remember that."

She said that to me. The day before she was arrested. She was on the porch. I had just finished dinner and walked outside. Momma looked like she had been crying. Of course she had been. She had her worried face. I didn't know why at the time. I thought it was because I was getting in trouble. But it was because of what she had done. Momma knew she had made a mistake. She knew she was caught. She shouldn't have stolen that money.

I watched the sunrise this morning. I woke up before dawn. The sun rises the way it sets. I mean the colors are the same. Just in reverse. Dark blue, light blue, orange. Just as nice. I thought of Momma. How she is in jail. How we are here, in foster care. I thought of you. And Vanessa and Sara. We are brothers. We should be together. We should have our sisters with us, too. I thought of

Dad and how I wish he was still alive.

I'm starting new, sort of. I've switched foster homes again. I didn't know why at first. I hadn't done anything wrong. The caseworker just called and told me to pack. Rachel looked sad about it. She said they had a family emergency. She and Lin couldn't take care of me anymore. The caseworker picked me up two days later.

You know what's funny? I actually got used to my last foster home. I was used to all the traffic. All the other foster kids. The animals, too. The weird food. Everything.

My new foster home is different. I'm the only foster kid. Paul and Avery (my new foster keepers) don't have kids. So it's just me. We live in an apartment downtown. I have my own room. It's quiet. It's always quiet. No one talks here!

It's not bad here though. Cleaner than most foster homes. Super-clean. Smells better. And there's a lot of food. Paul and Avery are much nicer than old Ms. Cutter. I don't have a ton of chores. They're not super-strict. They have a computer.

I do think it's weird that they don't have any mirrors! It's a little creepy, actually. And the only part I really hate is switching schools. I didn't have to before. But my new foster keepers are far. They're too far from my old school. Other than that, I can't complain. But I don't want to get too comfortable. I don't have much stuff. Some clothes. A pair of shoes. The camera Dad gave me. I can pack it all in a duffel bag.

Anyway.

How are things with your foster keepers? Did Susan and John have their baby? I know you were worried about it. I've told you many times. Don't get attached. Don't get comfortable.

Whoa, I just got a call. Just as I'm writing this email. Have you heard the news yet?

Momma is going to be released!! The

caseworker said in a month!

Don't be mad. Or disappointed in me. But I'm kind of worried.

We talked about this a lot. How much we want to be together. Now she will be coming home. Now it's finally here!

But I feel weird about it. About Momma being back.

Being separated was hard. Really hard. Especially in the beginning. Everything we've been through. And what about Vanessa and Sara?! What if she makes more mistakes? Big ones. Like the one that got her in jail. Don't get me wrong. I'm glad she's coming home. I want her home. I just don't ever want to go through…this. Ever again.

ABOUT THE AUTHOR

Cyn Bermudez is a writer from Bakersfield, California. She attended college in Santa Barbara, California, where she studied physics, film, and creative writing. Her work can be found in anthologies such as *Building Red: Mission Mars*, *The Best of Vine Leaves Literary Journal* (2014), and more. Her fiction and poetry can also be found in *Middle Planet*, *Perihelion SF*, *Strangelet*, *Mirror Dance*, and *805 Literary and Art Journal*, among others. For more information about Cyn, visit her website at www.cynbermudez.com.

BROTHERS

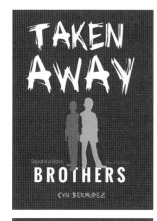

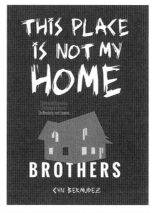

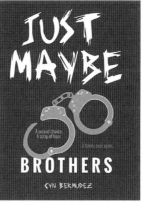

Check out more books at:
www.west44books.com